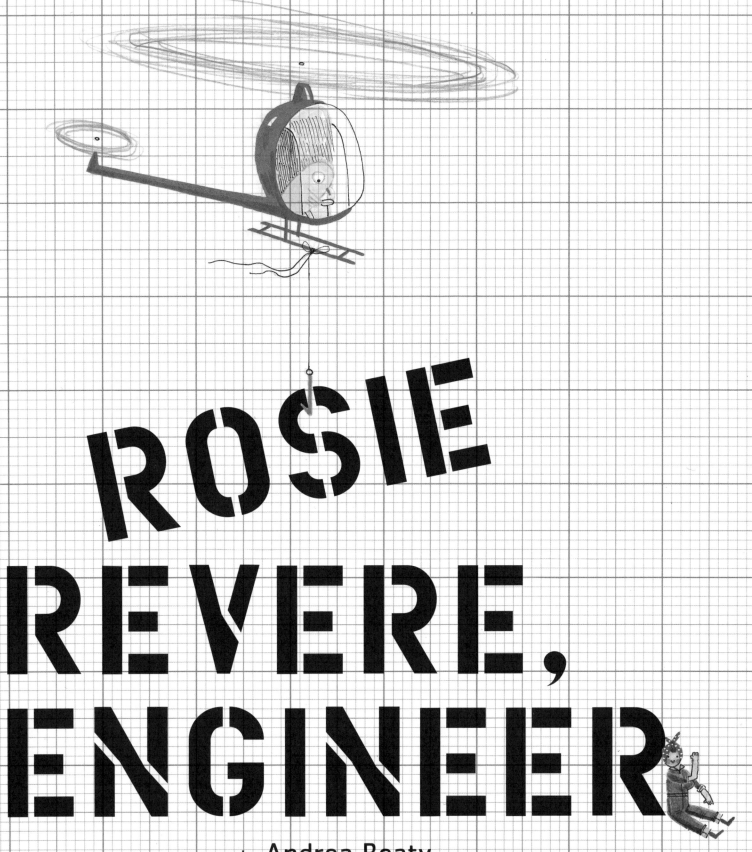

ROSIE REVERE, ENGINEER

by **Andrea Beaty**

illustrated by **David Roberts**

Abrams Books for Young Readers, New York

THIS IS THE STORY OF ROSIE REVERE,

who dreamed of becoming a great engineer.

In Lila Greer's classroom at Blue River Creek,

young Rosie sat shyly, not daring to speak.

But when no one saw her, she peeked in the trash

for treasures to add to her engineer's stash.

And late, late at night, Rosie rolled up her sleeves

and built in her hideaway under the eaves.

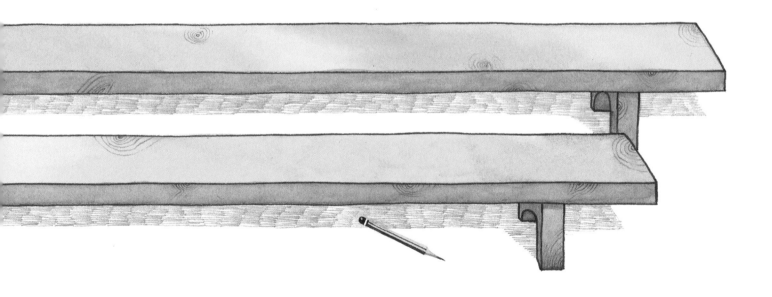

Alone in her attic, the moon high above,

dear Rosie made gadgets and gizmos she loved.

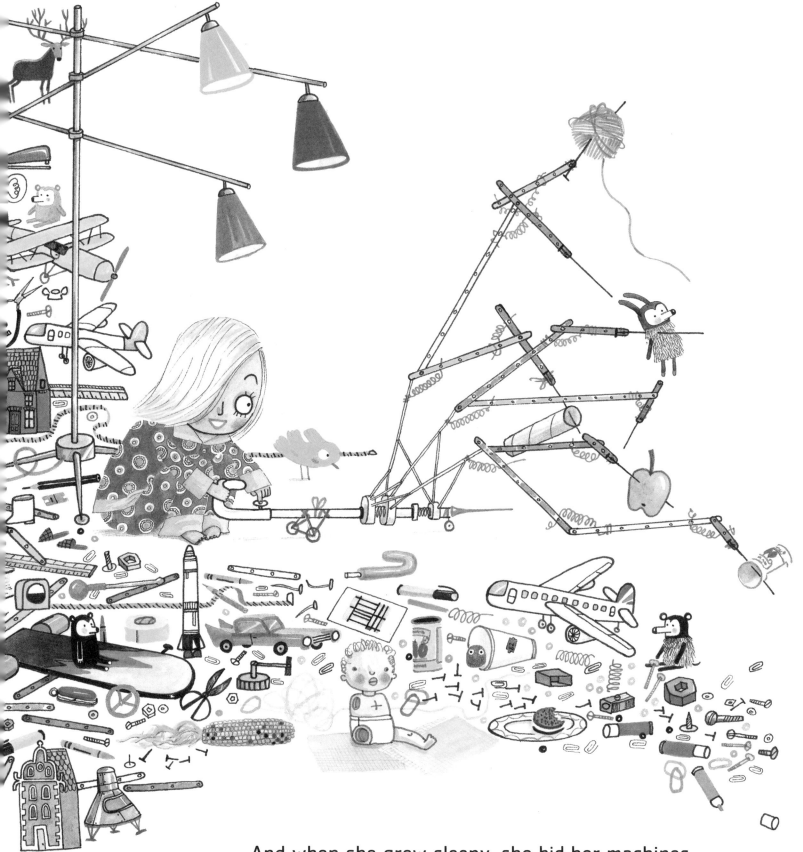

And when she grew sleepy, she hid her machines

far under the bed, where they'd never be seen.

When Rosie was young, she had not been so shy.

She worked with her hair swooping over one eye

and made fine inventions for uncles and aunts:

a hot dog dispenser and helium pants.

The uncle she loved most was Zookeeper Fred.

She made him a hat (to keep snakes off his head)

from parts of a fan and some cheddar cheese spray—

which everyone knows keeps the pythons away.

And when it was finished, young Rosie was proud,

but Fred slapped his knee and he chuckled out loud.

He laughed till he wheezed and his eyes filled with tears,

all to the horror of Rosie Revere,

who stood there embarrassed, perplexed, and dismayed.

She looked at the cheese hat and then looked away.

"I love it," Fred hooted. "Oh, truly I do."

But Rosie Revere knew that could not be true.

She stuck the cheese hat on the back of her shelf

and after that day kept her dreams to herself.

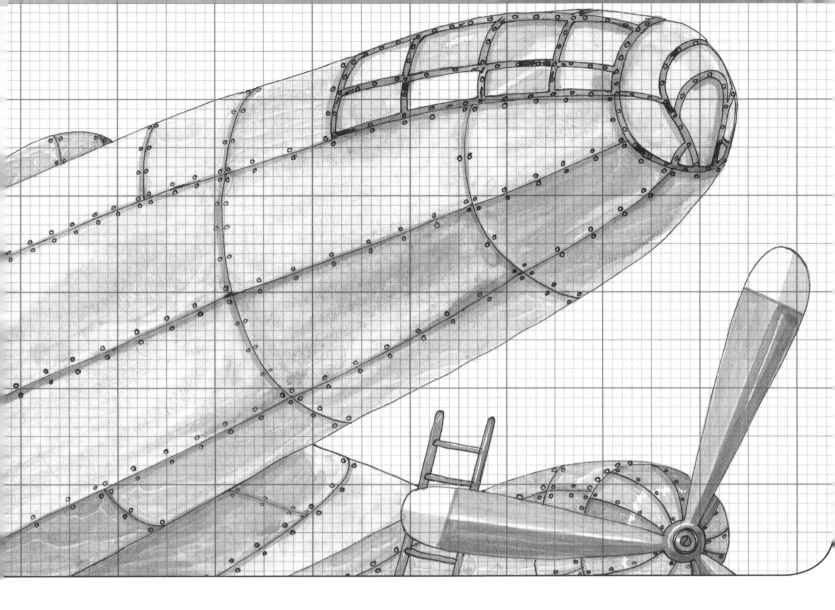

And that's how it went until one autumn day.

Her oldest relation showed up for a stay.

Her great-great-aunt Rose was a true dynamo

who'd worked building airplanes a long time ago.

She told Rosie tales of the things she had done

and goals she had checked off her list one by one.

She gave a sad smile as she looked to the sky:

"The only thrill left on my list is to fly!

But time never lingers as long as it seems.

I'll chalk that one up to an old lady's dreams."

That night, as Rosie lay wide-eyed in bed,

a daring idea crept into her head.

Could *she* build a gizmo to help her aunt fly?

She looked at the cheese hat and said, "No, not I."

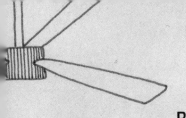

But questions are tricky, and some hold on tight,

and this one kept Rosie awake through the night.

So when dawn approached and red streaks lit the sky,

young Rosie knew just how to make her aunt fly.

She worked and she worked till the day was half gone,

then hauled her cheese-copter out onto the lawn

to give her invention a test just to see

the ridiculous flop it might turn out to be.

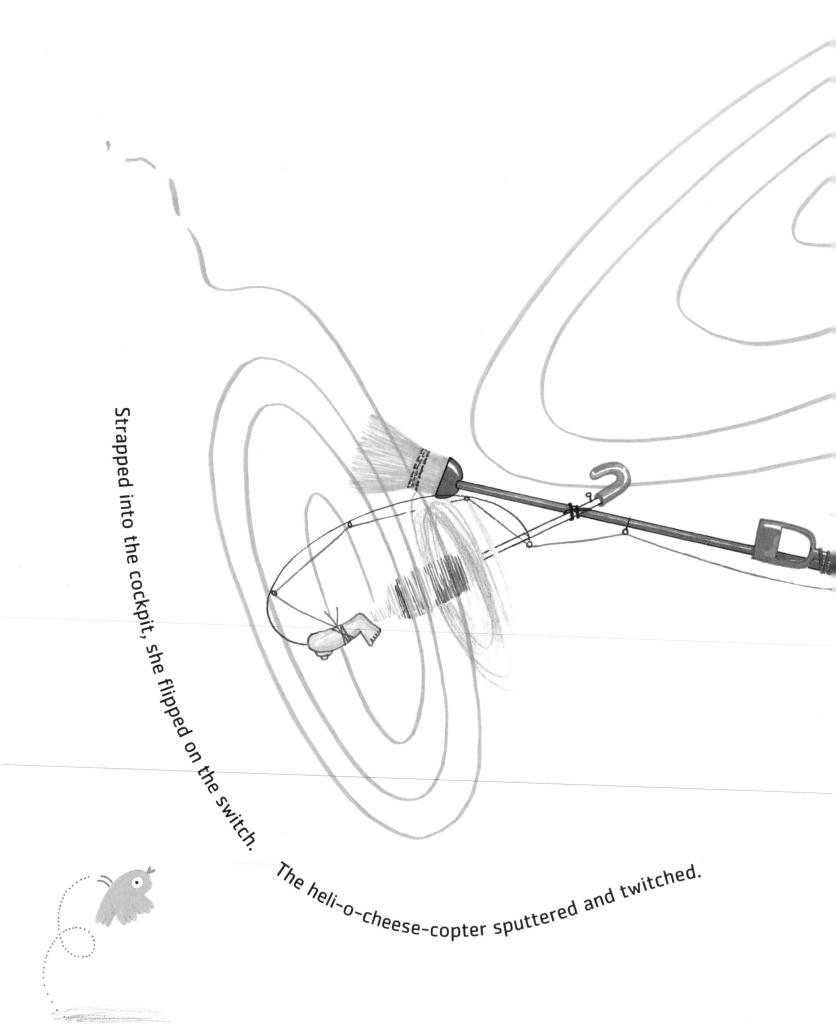

Strapped into the cockpit, she flipped on the switch.

The heli-o-cheese-copter sputtered and twitched.

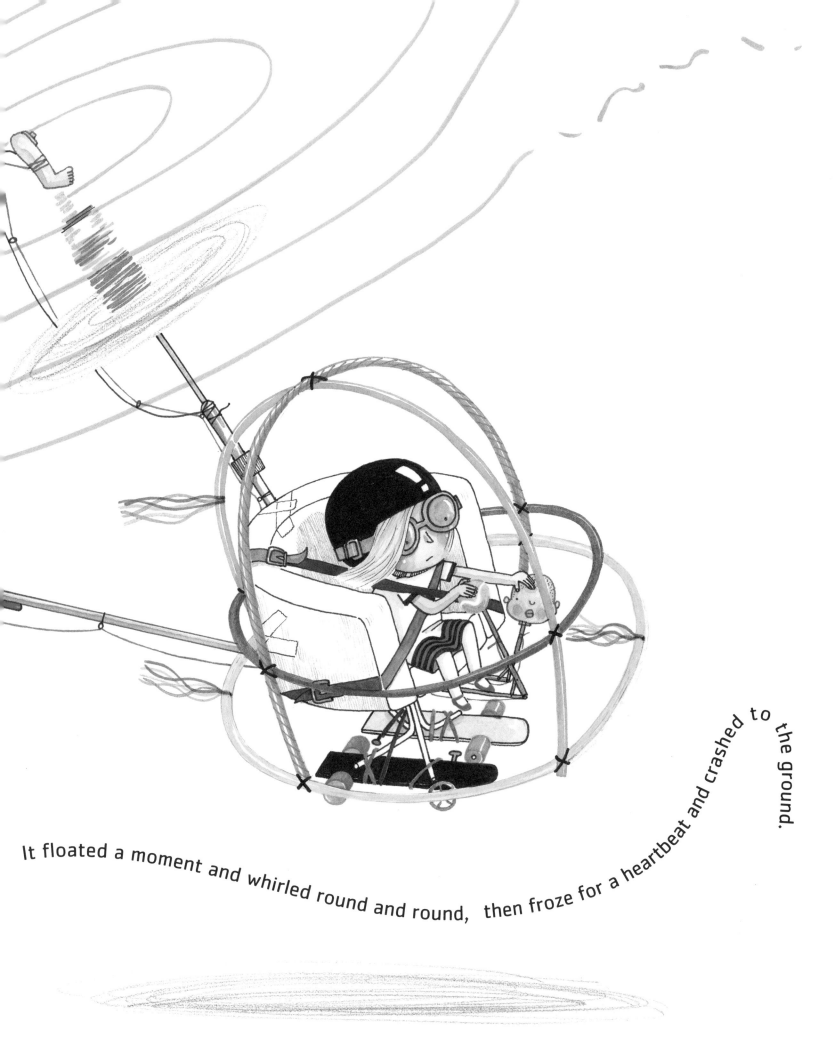

It floated a moment and whirled round and round, then froze for a heartbeat and crashed to the ground.

Then Rosie heard laughter and turned round to see

the old woman laughing and slapping her knee.

She laughed till she wheezed and her eyes filled with tears

all to the horror of Rosie Revere,

who thought, "Oh, no! Never! Not ever again

will I try to build something to sputter or spin

or build with a lever, a switch, or a gear.

And never will I be a great engineer."

She turned round to leave, but then Great-Great-Aunt Rose

grabbed hold of young Rosie and pulled her in close

and hugged her and kissed her and started to cry.

"You did it! Hooray! It's the perfect first try!

This great flop is over. It's time for the next!"

Young Rosie was baffled, embarrassed, perplexed.

"I failed," said dear Rosie. "It's just made of trash.

Didn't you see it? The cheese-copter crashed."

"Yes!" said her great aunt. "It crashed. That is true.

But first it did just what it needed to do.

Before it crashed, Rosie . . .

before that . . .

it flew!"

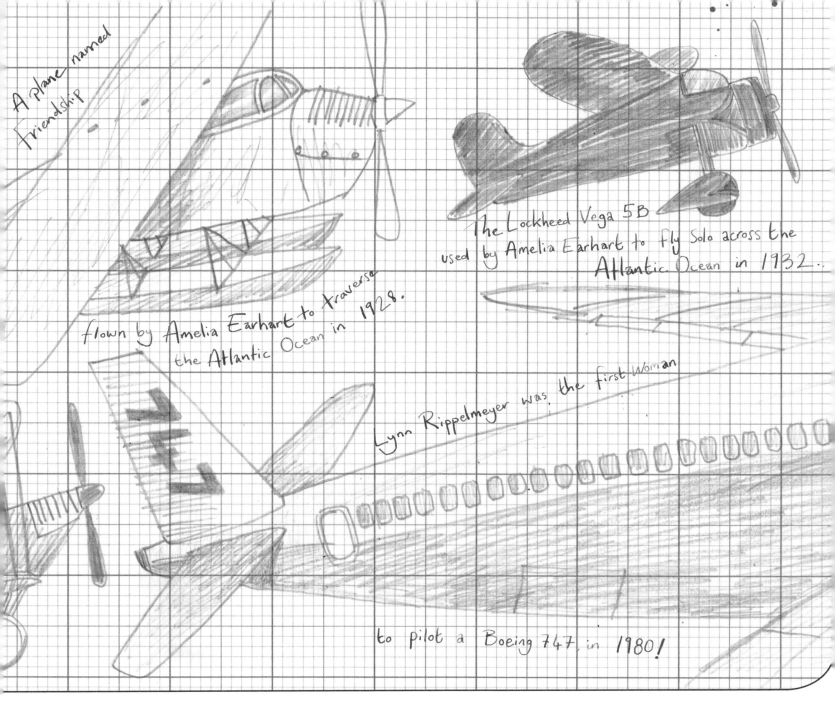

A plane named Friendship

The Lockheed Vega 5B used by Amelia Earhart to fly Solo across the Atlantic Ocean in 1932.

flown by Amelia Earhart to traverse the Atlantic Ocean in 1928.

Lynn Rippelmeyer was the first Woman

to pilot a Boeing 747, in 1980!

"Your brilliant first flop was a raging success!

Come on, let's get busy and on to the next!"

She handed a notebook to Rosie Revere,

who smiled at her aunt as it all became clear.

Life might have its failures, but this was *not* it.

The only true failure can come if you quit.

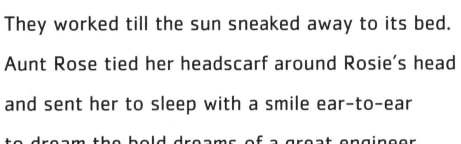

They worked till the sun sneaked away to its bed.

Aunt Rose tied her headscarf around Rosie's head

and sent her to sleep with a smile ear-to-ear

to dream the bold dreams of a great engineer.

At Blue River Creek all the kids in grade two

build gizmos and gadgets and doohickeys too.

With each perfect failure, they all stand and cheer,
but none quite as proudly as Rosie Revere.

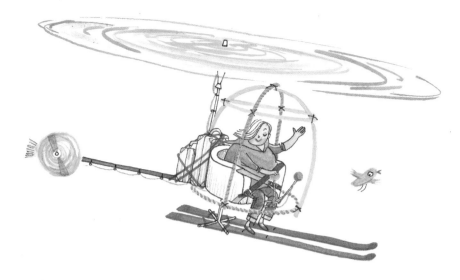

With gratitude to our parents' and grandparents' generation
for doing what was needed when it was needed the most
—A. B. & D. R.

HISTORICAL NOTE

During World War II, millions of women in the United States, the United Kingdom, Australia, Canada, New Zealand, the Soviet Union, and other allied nations worked to provide the food and equipment needed for the war effort. Some worked on farms to grow food for the troops. Others built ships, airplanes, tanks, and jeeps. With the help of many women, American factories produced more than three hundred thousand aircraft, eighty-six thousand tanks, and two million army trucks during the war. In the United States, these women were represented by Rosie the Riveter, the scarf-wearing fictional character whose slogan was "We can do it!"

The illustrations in this book were made with watercolors, pen, and ink on Arches paper. For some pieces, pencil and graph paper were also employed.

Cataloging-in-Publication Data has been applied
for and may be obtained from the Library of Congress.
ISBN: 978-1-4197-0845-9

Text copyright © 2013 Andrea Beaty
Illustrations copyright © 2013 David Roberts
Book design by Chad W. Beckerman

Printed and bound in U.S.A.
39 38 37 36 35 34 33

Abrams Books for Young Readers are available at special discounts when purchased in quantity for premiums and promotions as well as fundraising or educational use. Special editions can also be created to specification. For details, contact specialsales@abramsbooks.com or the address below.

ABRAMS The Art of Books
195 Broadway, New York, NY 10007
abramsbooks.com